SAM

and the
Seven-Pound Perch

written by

PAUL J. HOFFMAN

illustrated by

NICK PATTON

Sam and the Seven-Pound Perch
Written by Paul J. Hoffman © 2018

Printed in the United States of America

Illustrated by Nick Patton
Graphic design by Claire Flint Last

Luminare Press
438 Charnelton St., Suite 101
Eugene, OR 97401
www.luminarepress.com

ISBN: 978-1-944733-68-1

To kids everywhere (young and old)
who love to fish

My name is Sam and since I was a kid
I wanted to do what no other kids did.

Not a doctor, a teacher, or star on TV
A "fisherman" is what I wanted to be.

My first word wasn't "Mama," like most mothers wish.
What came out of my mouth wasn't "Dada," but **"FISH."**

I thought about fish from the time I could walk.
And drew pictures of fish with crayons and chalk.

When my Gramps took me fishing I really loved going.
I would sit next to him and help with the rowing.

My dog Jock came along whenever I went.
He would bark at the fish and sniff at their scent.

We fished only for perch which are usually small.
But when Gramps told a tale, it was usually tall.

Gramps said, "There's a seven-pound perch in our lake!
I once had him hooked, but I made a mistake."

"He bit on my worm on a bright summer day.
When I saw him and jerked the huge fish got away."

"It's your turn to catch the world-record perch."
So with Gramps' lucky hat, I started my search.

I fished the whole lake, and I tried every bait.
I learned where they lived and I learned what they ate.

I tried marshmallows, worms, night crawlers, too
Minnows and crayfish, to name just a few.

I fished through the ice in the cold and the snow.
I fished in the rain and got wet head to toe.

I didn't give up. I fished every day.
I fished shallow and deep, for hours I'd stay.

One morning at dawn with my faithful dog, Jock,
With some worms and my pole, we walked to the dock.

Jock jumped in the boat, and I rowed to the west
To my number one spot where the fishing was best.

The small perch were hungry, the fishing was great
But, my worms were all gone. I had run out of bait!

I knew that the seven-pound perch was down there.
I couldn't stop fishing, I just didn't dare.

Jock wanted to go in more ways than one,
And the next thing I knew, his squat had begun.

Jock pooped in the boat and I shouted, "Yuck!".
I couldn't believe I had so much bad luck.

Then a crazy idea came into my head.
If I don't have a worm, I'll try Jock's poop instead.

I picked up a chunk, it was warm and quite firm
And I thought, "Will it work just as good as a worm?"

"It's time to find out," I said with a smile.
"I'll give Jock's poop a try and fish for a while."

I was just about ready to give up and leave,
when my pole bent in half with a gigantic heave!

I set the hook hard and the monster swam deeper.
I knew in my heart that this fish was a keeper.

He wouldn't come up, tried to stay on the bottom.
I reeled really slow to make sure that I got him.

He finally got tired and came up at last.
When I saw him I gasped and my heart beat real fast.

All my life I had dreamed for this fish to appear.
It was the seven-pound perch! The victory was near!

I dipped in the net, caught the fish with one scoop.
It was just Jock and me, and a pile of poop!

Now that I caught him I should have been glad,
But the flopping big fish made me feel very sad.

If I took this fish home just to hang on the wall,
It wouldn't be right ... not right at all.

So I smiled and I told him, "It's your lucky day!"
Then I gently released him and he swam away.

Letting him go was the right thing to do.
I know he was happy and I felt good, too.

It isn't the trophy that's important to win
It's doing your best and to never give in.

I still love to fish, but only for fun.
And I'm proud of the wonderful thing I had done.

Now when I go I take Jock now and then,
but I'll never try fishing with dog poop again!

PERCH FACTS

- The Yellow Perch, or simply 'Perch' is a freshwater fish found only in North America.

- Adult perch range in size from 4-to- 12 inches, but are known to grow larger.

- Perch swim in schools of 50-200 fish to protect themselves from predators.

- Perch is one of the most popular species to fish for in the United States and Canada because it is easy to catch.

- Perch fishing is a great way for children to learn to fish.

- The world-record perch (18 inches long, weighing 4 pounds 3 ounces) was caught in New Jersey in 1865. It is the longest standing record for a freshwater fish in North America.

Was Sam's monster perch really seven pounds?
To Sam, it was!

Sam and the Seven-Pound Perch
READER'S GUIDE

FROM THE AUTHOR

I've had the pleasure of reading and discussing *Sam and the Seven-Pound Perch* with many groups of pre-kindergarten and elementary school children. The following guide offers suggestions and ideas that may be helpful when you read the book to them.

PRIOR TO READING THE STORY, I ASK AND SAY THE FOLLOWING:

Sam and the Seven-Pound Perch is a story about a boy named Sam who loves to go fishing.

* How many of you have gone fishing?

* Have you ever caught a perch?

Then I show the kids an illustration of the perch shown on the title page.

This is not just a book about fishing; it's also about determination and creativity.

* Do you know what the word determination means?

...*It's when you keep trying to do something that is hard to do and you never give up.*

* Do you know what the word creativity means?

...*It's making new things or thinking of new ideas.*

This is also a book about family, friendship, and doing the right thing. As you listen to the story about Sam, notice when you can see and hear about all of these things.

It's fun to talk about the the illustrations. Ask what they see on the page where Gramps is telling the story about the seven-pound perch. The kids often connect with the picture Sam painted at the end of the story. There are three baby perch in the painting... the perch had a family, too!

AFTER READING THE BOOK I ASK THE FOLLOWING:

* How was the story about determination?

* What did Sam try to do every day?

* How was the story about family?

* Who taught Sam how to fish?

* How was the story about friendship?

* Who was Sam's best friend?

* How was the story about creativity?

* What new idea did Sam have?

* How was the story about doing the right thing?

* What good choice did Sam make after catching the seven-pound perch?

* Why do you think he let the fish go?

* What did Sam do to remember catching the seven-pound perch?

* What did you like the most about the story?

Whether reading the book to a group of kids or to a child at bedtime, I hope you enjoy the story of Sam. Also, I am always grateful for positive online reader reviews if you feel so inspired.

Thank you!

PAUL J. HOFFMAN, the author
paulhoffman930@gmail.com

PAUL J. HOFFMAN, author

Paul Hoffman has always enjoyed poetry and story telling. 'Sam and the Seven Pound Perch' was written to entertain a group of young children (and their parents) during a family fishing vacation.

Paul stays young at heart tutoring elementary school students and spending 'Papa time' with his five grandchildren Sophie, Anna, Elena, Oliver, and Sam.

NICK PATTON, illustrator

Nick Patton loves stories. In addition to the role of dad, husband and son, Nick is an artist, illustrator and creator of the beloved Picturebooking Podcast.

Visit him online at
picturebooking.com

Made in the USA
Monee, IL
23 August 2022

12337708R00024